The House That Had Enough

By P. E. KING
Illustrated by JOHN O'BRIEN

A GOLDEN BOOK • NEW YORK
Western Publishing Company, Inc., Racine, Wisconsin 53404

Library of Congress Catalog Card Number: 85-51678 ISBN 0-307-10253-X/ISBN 0-307-68253-6 (lib. bdg.) C D E F G H I J

One morning, Anne woke up on the floor with a big BUMP!

Anne looked up. Her bed was standing over her.

"I've had enough," the bed said. "You never make me. You jump up and down on me. I'm going someplace where people will take better care of me."

Then the bed ran out of the room.

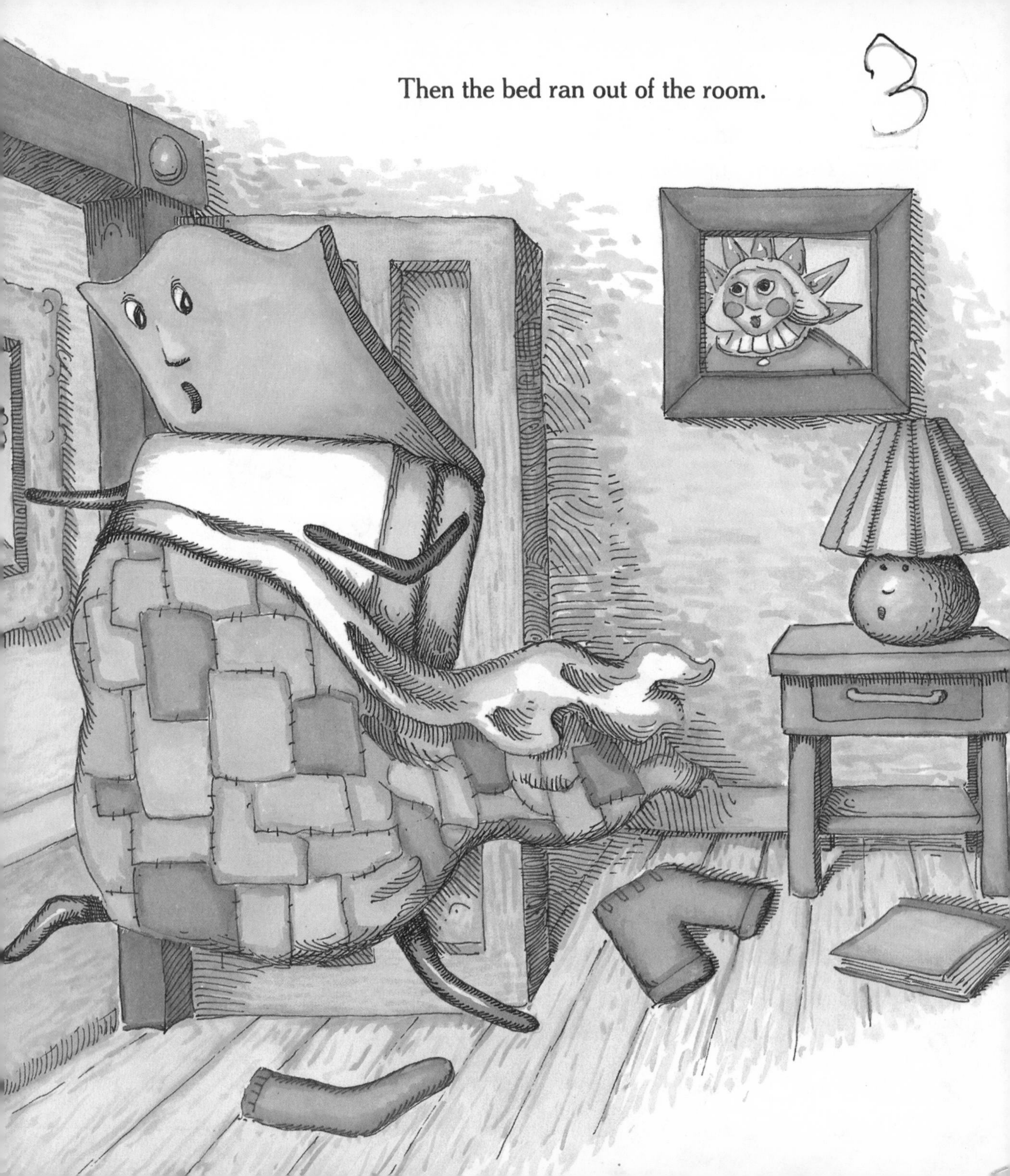

Anne was very surprised.

"What a strange way to start the day," she thought.

Suddenly Anne's dirty clothes stood up. Her favorite shirt said, "You wear us every day. You get us dirty and tear holes in us. You don't fold us or wash us. You just throw us on the floor. We've had enough, too. Let's go, clothes!"

The clothes ran out of the room.

Anne sat on the floor. Her pillow sat beside her.

"You've always been nice to me," the pillow said. "You hold me at night. I'll stay with you, Anne."

"Thank you," said Anne.

Anne went into the bathroom to brush her teeth.

But when she reached for her toothbrush, it jumped away.

"You don't rinse me out," said the toothbrush. "You leave little pieces of toothpaste in me."

The toothpaste added, "I get dry and crusty because you don't put my cap back on."

When Anne reached for the soap, it said, "You leave water in my dish. I'm soggy all the time!"

"You don't hang us up to dry after you use us," said the towels. "We're always damp."

And with that, the toothbrush, the toothpaste, the soap, and the towels ran out of the bathroom.

By this time Anne was getting hungry. She wanted breakfast. So she went into the kitchen to make a peanut butter-and-pickle sandwich.

But when Anne reached for the refrigerator door, the refrigerator jumped away.

"Anne," the refrigerator said, "you let milk spill in me. You leave the lid off the pickle jar. I smell terrible now. I'm leaving!"

Anne looked around the kitchen. The spoons, knives, forks, dishes, and glasses had lined up on the floor.

"I suppose you're leaving, too," Anne said.

"You never wash us after you use us," said one of the spoons. "We just can't take it anymore!"

They all ran out.

Anne sat down next to her pillow.
"What next?" she asked.

Just then, Anne's favorite doll walked by. She pulled Anne's other toys in a wagon.

"You don't put us away," the doll said. "We get stepped on. It just isn't safe here."

The doll ran out the front door, pulling the wagon behind her.

Anne followed her doll to the door and looked out.

She saw her hammer running off. It called to Anne, "You used me to hammer the sidewalk!"

Anne saw the garbage cans, her bike, and a can of paint following the hammer.

"You pound us like drums," the garbage cans said.

"You ride me down the stairs," the bike said.

"You used me to paint the front lawn," the can of paint said.

Anne and her pillow went outside and watched the hammer and the can of paint disappear around the corner.

Suddenly there was a loud CRUNCH! Anne turned around.

Her house was standing up!

"You slam my doors when you're angry," the house said. "You leave my windows open when it rains. You hang posters on my walls with pins. Well, young lady, this house has had quite enough!"

"I had no idea everything was so mad at me," Anne said. "I can take better care of my things. Honest!"

"She can!" the pillow added.

"Well, I do feel kind of empty now that all your things have left," the house said. "Maybe I can talk them into coming back. But first, promise me you'll take better care of us."

"I promise!" shouted Anne.

"I'll see what I can do," said the house, and it ran off.

A little while later, the house returned with Anne's things inside it.

"Now do as you promised," the house said.

"I will!" Anne shouted. "Thank you, house. You won't regret this."

She ran inside.

Anne cleaned the refrigerator.
She washed the dishes.

Anne put the cap on the toothpaste.

She rinsed out her toothbrush.

Anne folded her clothes and put them away.

She made her bed.

She put her toys away.

She was busy all day long. Now it was time for bed.

Anne curled up in her warm bed. She looked around her neat, clean room.

"Isn't it great to have everything back?" she asked her pillow.

The pillow smiled and said, "It sure is, Anne. Good night, and sleep well!"

And Anne did.